Lusting

After

Valentine

Helen Walton

Walton House Publishing

Contents

A Short Story	1
Afterword	37
Acknowledgments	39
Also By	41
About Author	43

A Short Story

♥

THEY'D VOTED VALENTINE D. Ross sexiest man alive for the second year running. If I was the one running the contest, he'd win every year. He was without a doubt the most stunning man on Earth. Not just my opinion. Women everywhere swooned over Valentine's dark hair and blue eyes. He also sported a rock-hard chest, which he flaunted without a care in the world to the many paparazzi who followed him. Pictures of him graced the internet every day.

Not that I was a stalker or anything. A little obsessed. Maybe. Okay. A lot. But my lucky duck of a sister acted opposite him every day in the famous television show Cupid's

Arrow. A show which made Valentine and my sister, Olive Sanchez, famous for their on-screen chemistry. To say I was jealous was an understatement. But then my sister always had more luck than me in everything. From jobs to boyfriends, not that she and Valentine were dating. Thank the heavens for that minor miracle. Otherwise, I might die from the green-eyed monster clawing my insides whenever she talked to me about Valentine. Which was way too often and yet not enough.

"Hazel, are you still there?" Olive huffed.

"Yes." I doodled a heart on the notepad with a red pen.

"Did you hear what I said?"

"Um." I wrote Valentine's initials inside the heart.

Olive sighed, long and loud. So loud I dropped the pen.

"What's up?" I asked.

"I broke my arm."

"What? No way!" I sat up and thrust the notepad across the desk. "How did you do that?"

"I already told you, but you weren't listening."

"My bad." I rustled the pile of script papers. "I'm reading through lines for an audition and my mind was elsewhere."

"Is the little Australian country Christmas play finished?"

"Well, it is the new year," I said ladling on the sarcasm.

"I have a job for you here in America."

"I don't want to come home." My petulance whined in my voice.

"Even though the ass of a donkey you called a boyfriend dumped you the moment you stepped foot in his country?"

I scrunched up the paper with my doodle. "I'm having fun in Australia, and I've made friends."

"You'll make friends here too. It wouldn't be like moving back to Pittsburgh."

"And why would I move to Georgia?"

"For crying out loud. Do you ever listen?" She cursed under her breath for a solid minute. "I broke my arm. In a motorbike accident. The production company is looking for a body double for some of my scenes. They toyed with the idea of writing my broken arm into the show but decided to go against it. Anyway..."

"Anyway, what?" I threw the ball of paper in the wastebasket's direction. It bounced off the rim and landed on the floor.

"Anyway, I told them you're a perfect stunt double for me since we're sisters and we have the same coloring."

I stepped over to the bin and gathered the paper. "You want me to be your stunt double? But you don't do stunts. It's all smooching and sex scenes."

"Correct."

The ball of paper fell from my suddenly lifeless fingers. My mind couldn't get over the images of me and Valentine in smooching scenes. Sex scenes. Icy coldness skated over my skin while my insides warmed.

"The damn cast gets in the way. There's nothing sexy about it at all and you see what our fans are like. As if we can cut those scenes for eight weeks. Will you do it?"

"Will I come to Georgia and act as your double in sex scenes with Valentine D. Ross?" I gaped at the absurdity of the question. As if I'd say no.

Olive's throaty laugh echoed down the line. "I'll take that as a yes."

"Yes, yes, yes. I'll see when the next flight is."

"I have you booked on the flight out tomorrow. Check your email for your itinerary."

"You were sure I'd say yes?"

"I knew my sister would come to my rescue."

"Ha. You realize it's all about Valentine."

She giggled. "It's going to be fun watching you pretend to act with Valentine."

"Hey, I'm a complete professional. Just because I haven't got my big break like you yet doesn't mean I can't act."

She made kissing noises.

"Oh, shut up." I hung up on her.

Stupid older sisters thought they knew everything. She might, but I wouldn't give her an even bigger head. I surveyed my tiny bedroom in the hotel I'd been using while staying in Newberry. I wouldn't miss the cramped space or the hot, dry summer heat, the endless flies, or the dust. Australia had been a wonderful adventure. I'd miss Candy, though. Now she had her super-hot boyfriend, Devin. I could at least leave knowing she had her happily ever after with the man she'd lusted after for four years.

I hadn't lusted after Valentine for that long, but it sure seemed like years.

I was due to meet up for drinks with Candy and Devin at the local pub tonight. Who would have thought this would be my going home party? I'd keep in contact with Candy, but it wouldn't be the same. Maybe one day she'd visit me in Georgia. Since she and Devin were both actors, and Devin would head back to Hollywood theaters soon, it was likely Candy would follow him to America too. If I stayed there after Olive's arm mended, that is. Eight weeks until she'd get the cast off. Eight weeks of being her stunt double for sex scenes.

Sounded like heaven to me.

"No, no, no," the director yelled. "You're doing it all wrong again." He threw his hands up in the air and stormed off the set.

"I'm sorry," I whispered.

Valentine sat up on the bed, his spectacular abs rippling for a beneficial effect on my raging libido. "It's not just you."

What I'd thought would be fun and hot turned out to be awful and awkward. I'd never acted in sex scenes before. This was an eye-opener. The bright lights bearing down on my almost naked skin and making beads of sweat drip from my pores with zero exertion. The crowd of stagehands looking on with beady eyes. Nothing about the scene was sexy at all.

How ridiculous I couldn't fake it with the Hollywood star voted the sexiest man of the year.

I sighed and hugged my knees to my chest.

Valentine ran his observant gaze over my forlorn face. I couldn't even meet his concerned eyes. I chewed my lip.

Olive stomped onto the bedroom set. "Hazel, I thought you could do this."

"Me too," I said.

She slid onto the bed beside me and wrapped her arm around my shoulders. Valentine escaped. I didn't blame him. Our on-stage acting together was appalling. It was like two clueless teenagers trying to get it on.

"Now he's gone. Tell me now if this is too much for you and we'll call it quits before you get fired."

"They're going to fire me?" I dropped my chin to my knees.

"If you can't act, then yes, they will."

"I can act," I mumbled. "It just feels awkward." I let go of my legs and waved my hands at the set, the people bustling around the room, the microphones, and the cameras.

"Look," she whispered, moving closer to my ear. "Stop thinking of Valentine as this famous, gorgeous actor and treat him like an ordinary man."

"Easy for you to say. You've been acting with him since before you both became famous."

"This is true. I appreciate how ordinary he is." She stood up. "Now, how do I look for the Valentine's Day party?"

Olive spun. She'd wrapped her voluptuous form in a sleek red sheath dress and on her head, she wore a tiny gold halo.

As if she were an angel.

"Nice." I smirked, knowing the one-word compliment would annoy her.

She quirked an eyebrow.

I giggled. "You're stunning, but you realize that. Plus, you should wear devil's horns, not an angel halo."

"I'll save the devil costume for Halloween." She grinned. "Are you sure you don't want to come with me?"

"I'm sure. I'm still catching up on the jet lag."

"Okay. Well, I'll see you whenever I get home."

"I'll see you for breakfast then?"

She flipped me the finger and strode away like she owned the place, her long deep brown hair swaying in time to her full hips. Sassy woman that she was. And so was I. If I could stop my insides flipping and my body igniting by Valentine's mere presence, that is.

I slithered off the bed and made my way to the dressing room. I stared in the mirror for a stupid amount of time, comparing myself to my sister. True, we both had the same bronzed complexion, same deep brown hair falling in soft waves to our hips, but our eyes were different colors. My eyes were blue with tiny flecks of hazel, while Olive's eyes were hazel with flecks of amber. Everyone thought it was hilarious my eyes weren't hazel when that was my name. The joke was on them. I didn't care. I ran a finger over my hip, the last place Valentine had touched in our acting sex scene. His touch had been electrifying. It'd taken all my concentration to not rub myself against him in a wanton way.

A sigh filled my lungs. What would it be like if Valentine touched me more, let alone placed his mouth on me as they'd written in the script? Except we didn't get to that part because I'd frozen like a naïve schoolgirl with a silly crush.

Maybe I wasn't a talented actor after all. I sniffed back my despair. If they fired me from this job, then I'd have to go home to Pennsylvania. Back to the place where my best friend and ex-boyfriend had hooked up behind my back and were now engaged to be married. Yeah, I don't think so. Wherever I traveled from here, it wouldn't be back home. If I did, I'd end up in jail for forcing them both to eat poop and apologize to me. Which neither had the integrity to do. The pair deserved each other.

I wriggled into my tight-fitting dress in a cream pleated material. The off the shoulder style and color highlighted my bronzed skin. The zipper running from top to bottom was more of an accessory than a way to get the dress on and off. Although I could use it for that purpose, I'd found it easier to wriggle it on and slide my arms into the long sleeves than to put my arms in the sleeves and zip it up. I brushed my hair back into a sleek ponytail, slid hoops into my earlobes, and gathered up my purse.

Flicking off the light switch, I opened the door and stepped out into the gloomy interior of the production studio. It was different without the bright lights and people bustling around. I frowned as I noted the complete absence of a single person. Had I stared in the mirror that long? I didn't think so, but my mind drifted sometimes. Anything was possible.

Mom called me a daydreamer. Dad called me his *cielito*, meaning his *little sky* because I was always floating away in it. Olive called me loco. Sisters could be the pits while being the best.

My heels clicked across the concrete floor as I made my way to the door. There was only the bright green exit light shining my way and a couple of smaller safety lights with a golden hue. The interior was cooler without the bright lights. Softer. Almost romantic. My gaze skittered to the bed.

"Argh!" I screamed, slamming both hands over my chest.

Valentine placed one arm behind his head while reclining on the bed. His gaze hooded under his half-closed eyelids.

"Wh... at..." I gasped for breath. "Are you doing laying there?"

"Waiting for you," he drawled. "Didn't realize I'd be waiting this long."

"I wasn't that long." I flicked my ponytail over my shoulder.

"Everyone else has left for the day."

"Perhaps they were eager to leave. It is Valentine's Day." I plonked my hands on my hips, suddenly defensive in front of this sexy man.

He patted the bed. "Come here. We need to talk."

I walked back toward the bed, my heart tripping over itself in an unnatural rhythm at being alone with Valentine D. Ross. The sexiest man alive. All to myself. A bed. Alone.

Get your mind out of the bedroom.

"I'm sorry about today. I'll do better tomorrow, I promise."

"It's been days, Hazel. If we haven't found our groove by now, I'm not sure we will."

"Are you firing me?" I sucked in a breath to stop from breaking down in sobs.

"No." He patted the bed. "I think we need to work on this together without the distraction of the camera and crew."

"Oh." I placed my bag on the end of the bed. "Good idea."

"Yeah, I thought so."

He sat up at the same time as I sat down. His fingers toyed with the ends of my ponytail and sent tiny shivers of delight down my spine. I stared straight ahead, not willing to let him see how he turned me on with such ease.

How hard it was to act like his touch didn't set me on fire.

"You're exquisite, Hazel."

"Thanks," I said. "I look a lot like my sister."

"You do and you don't. You have this little mark here." He touched a spot on my shoulder. "She doesn't."

"No, she doesn't." I shivered.

He stroked the spot with his finger. "It makes me want to kiss it."

"I..." I licked my lips.

"You?" He dipped his head forward to peer into my eyes.

Was he about to kiss me? For real? Or acting?

I stood up with a start, smacking my head into his on the way up.

"What the ever-living?" he groaned, rubbing his forehead.

"I'm sorry," I said for the umpteenth time, holding my head.

I'd cherish the lump on my head. Put a sign around it saying the Valentine D. Ross gave it to me. I groaned at myself and my craziness. I trotted across the room and flung open the exit door, escaping before I humiliated myself even further.

Damn attractive man.

Damn my childish hormones.

I was twenty-six, not sixteen. You wouldn't tell by the way I'd acted. Acting. Gah. I spluttered obscenities to the night sky.

A loud masculine laugh rumbled behind me.

I spun around.

"You forgot your purse."

He dangled my bag from his fingers. I grabbed at it, but he lifted it out of reach.

"Why are you jumpy around me?" His eyebrows dipped in a question.

"I'm not."

"Are too."

I huffed. Now I'd made him act like a teenager.

"This is getting us nowhere," I pointed out.

"You don't like me, do you?" he asked.

"I like you," I spluttered. As if any woman wouldn't like him.

"We only met three days ago."

"Perhaps, but Olive talks about you all the time."

His gorgeous, kissable pink lips spread into a grin.

"Olive talks about me?" He tilted his head.

Did he have the hots for my sister? Is that why they could act out sex scenes with such ease? And now I was in the way? My fingers curled into my palms. She just had to have everything, didn't she? While leaving me with her crumbs.

I stomped across the parking lot.

"Hazel, wait." Valentine caught up to me. "How are you getting home?"

"I'll catch an Uber."

"Let me drive you."

"Olive won't be there. She's out at a Valentine's Day party. I doubt she'll be home before the sun."

"What's Olive got to do with me driving you home?" His perfect dark brows dipped between his eyes.

"I wanted you to know so you could take back your offer."

"Why would I take back my offer?" His frown dipped lower.

I inhaled a deep breath and let it out. "Look, just tell Olive you like her."

He threw his head back and roared with laughter. As he wiped the laughter tears from the corners of his eyes, he said, "I don't like Olive like that. She's a talented actress and makes work fun, but there'll never be more between us."

"Oh." I snatched my bag from his hands and clenched it to my chest. "But you were happy she talked about you to me."

His lips spread into a swoon-worthy grin. "Because she talks to me about you all the time. It feels like I know you."

I dipped my chin as warmth filled my cheeks.

"Are you blushing?"

"What? No." I turned my head away, but there was no hiding the fact I was blushing.

"You are too." He chuckled. "It's sweet."

"Sweet?" I shifted back to face him.

"Like a piece of candy."

I giggled. "I have a friend named Candy."

"I know."

My eyebrows rose. "How much has Olive told you about me?"

"How much has she told you about me?"

"Good point." I smirked. "Okay, you can drive me home."

"It would be my pleasure." He waved his hand toward a solitary car in the parking lot.

A dark-gray Nissan 350z sports car that blended into the shadows of the twilight evening.

"Cute car," I said.

"Cute?" He placed both hands on his chest. "You wound my heart, sweet lady."

"Sorry," I drawled. "A woman should never attack a man's masculinity."

His perfect smile met mine over the top of the sports car.

"I see your sister was right about your humor."

"I can't believe she's been talking to you about *me*," I said.

He unlocked the car, and we climbed in.

"Why wouldn't she? She loves you and missed you while you were in Australia."

"You really are just friends with her?"

"Yes." He rolled his eyes. "Not all co-stars hook up."

"Of course. I'm sorry."

"No, it's okay. Everyone knows I dated my last co-star from the movie. Huge mistake and I've learned my lesson."

"I'm sorry."

"What for? It wasn't your fault she used me to hide the fact she was dating a slimy married rockstar." He wound down the window and hit the button to open the large wrought-iron gates to the production studio.

"I understand all about two-timing, back-stabbing, lying, cheating..."

His roar of laughter was infectious, and I laughed along with him.

"Where's home?" he asked.

"You've never been to my sister's apartment?"

"No, we chat at work."

"Do you know where the Midtown Atlanta is?"

He nodded and set off down the road through the night-time traffic. Pretty lights lit up the surrounding buildings in the purple-gray sky as the sun made its descent for another day. Georgia sure was a pretty state.

"It's across the street from where I'm staying in the Iconic Midtown."

"How about that?"

"Small world." He winked.

"You may as well park at your place and I'll walk across the road," I said as the tall apartment building came into view.

My sister picked a great place to stay in Georgia, and at least her apartment had two bedrooms, so we wouldn't cramp each other's style for the next eight weeks. Not that I had a style. Not like Olive, who was all about fashion. I needed to stop comparing myself to my sister. We both had our positives and negatives. It was hard, though, coming back to America. I'd been myself in Australia. Here, I wasn't sure where I fit in.

Valentine killed the engine inside the parking garage and turned to me. "Would you like to have a drink with me?"

"Oh, I don't know." I met his sparkling blue eyes. "Don't you have a hot date for Valentine's Day?"

"No date." His chin dipped, and he peered up at me with puppy dog eyes. If dogs had blue eyes, that is. "Yet."

I sucked in a breath. "Are you asking me on a date?" I shook my head at how absurd I sounded.

"Yeah, I am."

"Why?" I whispered.

"Because I'm infatuated with you. Your sister built you up inside my head into this living, stunning, charming woman, and I can't stop thinking about you. When she said you were coming to Georgia, I thought all my wishes had come true. But meeting you made me realize they aren't true. Not yet, anyway." His tongue slid across his bottom lip.

I inched closer as though an invisible force drove me, but it was the force of me. Olive had done the same thing with him to me. It wasn't a crush from staring at his gorgeous pictures online, although I did that too. It was from all the words she'd said to me about him.

His gaze dipped to my lips. My breath stuttered in my lungs.

"Will you have a drink with me?" His voice came out soft and seductive.

"Yes." My voice echoed his.

His head inched closer until we were breathing the same air. The allure of his musky aftershave drifted closer and closer still as our lips almost touched.

"Can I kiss you?" he asked.

"Yes." I all but panted the word.

Valentine's lips skated over mine as though I'd burn him with the heat of my lips. With the warmth coming from inside me, it was possible. A tiny whimper of need escaped my mouth. His lips slanted over mine in a kiss that left me hungry no more. He consumed me with his lips. Devoured me with his tongue.

Our hands tugged at each other's clothing. His mouth obliterated any rational thought. I blazed in hunger. Consumed with need, I didn't register where we were or even cared in the slightest we were in his car getting it on like crazy teenagers. I wrenched his t-shirt up at the same time as his hand cupped my breast over the material of my dress. My nipple hardened in an instant, demanding more from him. Much more. His fingers dipped to the top of the zipper and dragged it down. I thanked the designer for making it this way before I slid my hand lower to the waistband of his jeans, stroking the indents on either side of his stomach. My mouth hungered to lick them, to taste him, but I couldn't give up the rapture of his mouth on mine.

He cupped my breasts while his fingers toyed with my nipples, then he broke the kiss to suckle and nuzzle my chest. I threw my head back and let him have them. His lips were warm, his tongue sure against my nipples with each hard tug. He drew one, then the other, into his mouth. I wrenched his zipper down and wrapped my palm around his hard cock. He let out a groan around my nipple, then he shoved my hand away, fished out his wallet, and rolled on a condom. I watched, enthralled for all thirty seconds, before his fingers dipped under my dress, tugged my panties to the side, and tested my wetness.

My slick arousal met his firm fingers. He thrust one finger inside me, then two, his thumb rubbing my clit in fast, firm strokes.

"Oh, Valentine," I moaned, gripping his shoulders tight.

He withdrew his fingers, making me pout. He smirked, pulling me on to his lap before bringing the tip of his hard cock to my dripping entrance. I lowered myself onto him, keeping our gazes locked as I slid down until I'd fully seated myself on his hard length. This moment here was like a dream. The sexiest man alive was inside me. He made me crazy, like a horny teenager.

"Hazel, sweet, I'm going to fuck you now."

"Yes, please," I whimpered.

He groaned, gripping my hips and guiding them up and down.

I followed his lead and plunged up and down his hard cock in a hectic rhythm that had us both panting for air in record time. Together, we moaned. Groaned. Sweated. Experienced everything as one. His solid thrusts ignited the bundle of nerves buried deep inside while the grind of his pelvis against mine rubbed my clit until it throbbed for release. But on and on, we screwed like teenagers. Hard and fast. Rocking the car and fogging up the windows with each frantic breath until each drag of his cock became too much pleasure. My legs quivered along with my insides. Pulse pounding in my ear, Valentine grew harder still inside me and I came in a rocking and rolling release against him.

"Hazel."

He groaned in my ear, dragged me to his chest, and exploded in orgasm with me.

His cock pulsed in time with my inner contractions. A reminder Valentine was mine for this short space in time. I slumped against him. My muscles were so lax, that they could no longer hold me. His hands shifted to my face. He cupped both cheeks and lifted my head to kiss my lips in the sweetest kiss ever. I smiled against his lips. He smiled back too and gazed into my eyes.

A bright flash of headlights flickered across us. I scrambled back to my seat, yanked up the zipper on my dress, and hunkered down so whoever had arrived in the parking garage wouldn't see me. Valentine zipped up his pants and shot me a huge grin.

"How about a drink now?"

A laugh bubbled freely from my lips. "Are you inviting me up to your apartment for a drink or more sex?"

"A little from column A, a lot from column B."

"How could a woman say no?" I drawled.

"True," he said. "It's not every day you get invitations from the sexiest man alive."

I leaned across the car and planted a kiss on his lips. He kissed me back, deepening the kiss until I squirmed with arousal once again. I planted both hands on his chest and pushed back.

"Okay, Valentine. I'll come up for a drink but..."

"You're not going to say no sex, are you?"

"No. I'm crazy, but I'm not insane." I chuckled. "But how about we tell each other a few of the things my sister has told us? That way, it will be real."

"This is as real as it gets, sweet."

"Aww, you're a sweetheart, too." I pecked a kiss on his lips.

His dark brows dipped into a frown. "Don't go ruining my reputation."

"What reputation? The sexiest man alive? How could I ruin that?"

His deep laugh filled the car. "I love your humor."

I flashed him a grin.

He ran a finger over my lips. "I love these lips. They taste better than candy."

I rolled my eyes. "Come on, sweet talker. Show me your apartment."

"Sure thing, sweet. Then I intend to find out if every part of your body is as delicious as candy."

He instantly filled my body with desire, but every part of me wanted this. Wanted Valentine. If we'd come together so crazy and fast, then surely this was meant to be?

"Well, well, well," Olive drawled. "Look who's coming home when the sun's coming up."

I flipped her the finger, kicked off my shoes at the door, and threw my bag on the hallway table.

"Dare I ask where you were all night?" She quirked an eyebrow. "And with whom?"

I collapsed on the couch beside her and rested my head on her shoulder. "Valentine."

"Yes," she shrieked and rubbed her hands together.

"Wait," I said, sitting up. "Did you plan this?"

She held her finger and thumb apart a fraction. "I may have played a small part in it."

I narrowed my eyes. "Is your arm even broken?"

"Of course it is. Do you like him?"

"I wouldn't have slept with him if I didn't like him."

"Hussy." She smirked.

"Tramp," I tossed back.

"I'll have you know I was home in bed before twelve, unlike some people."

"I was in bed before twelve."

"Not yours." She cackled.

I stomped into the bathroom and shut the door. Taking a quick shower since we were due at work in half an hour, I scrubbed Valentine's scent from my body, wishing I didn't have to.

Olive banged on the door. "Let's go."

"Coming," I hollered.

I dressed as fast as I could and raced out of the steaming bathroom. Olive continued smiling her shit-eating grin the entire time she drove us to the studio. We parted ways the second we stepped inside. I watched as she and Valentine did their scenes. Then it was time for our sex scene.

A unique set of nerves filled my body as I lay on the bed beside Valentine.

He smiled down at me. "Hi."

"Hi," I whispered.

"Action," the director yelled.

Valentine dipped his mouth below my ear. "Relax, sweet."

My body flared to life back in his arms, back with his lips on my body, his fingers tracing my limbs. I mirrored his actions. We kept the touching PG-rated, but I grew so hot, that an inferno blazed inside me.

"Cut," the director yelled.

I sat up, blinking against the brightness of the lights and trying to ignore the curious glances of the crew.

The director made his way to the bed. "That was perfect, you two. All wrapped up in one take. Well done."

"Thanks," I said, feeling like a total fraud since I hadn't acted for one second on the stage bed with Valentine.

I scampered off to the dressing room, leaving the director and Valentine talking. I sagged against the door as fraud kept flashing inside my mind. A knock against the timber made me jump and fling the door open before I'd even dressed. Valentine stood on the other side, dressed, of course, and oozing the sexiest man alive aura.

And he'd been mine last night.

He stepped inside and closed the door behind him.

"About last night," he said.

"You don't want to do it again." I straightened my spine against the onslaught of emotions.

"What?" He scowled. "Is that what you want?"

"Me?"

"Yes, what do you want?"

I ducked my chin. He stepped closer until his feet were almost touching mine.

"Hazel, sweet. I want you. What we shared last night was fast, and hot, but also gentle and real. If you used me for a one-night stand, then I understand. I've been there before. I won't be angry, but it will disappoint me."

I gasped and jerked my chin up. "Valentine, no. This was never about one night."

"Good." He held his arms open.

I stepped into them and wrapped my arms around his waist. His hands clasped my back in a comforting hug.

"I want you too, Valentine D. Ross." I lifted my face to his. "What does the D stand for?"

"It's a secret. If I tell you, then you'll have to keep it."

"I promise to never tell a soul."

"Dick."

"Dick what?" I frowned.

"D stands for Dick."

"Oh." I giggled.

"See, laughing is the reaction I don't want." His lips firmed. "Could you imagine how many people would make fun of me for having the name Dick?"

"People are horrible." I nodded while fighting more giggles.

"Tell me one of your secrets now."

"Hmm." I ran my hands over his chest. "I wasn't acting out there today."

His perfect, kissable lips spread into a sultry smile. "Are you saying if I dip my fingers inside your panties, I'll find you wet?"

"That's exactly what I'm saying."

"Good."

His hand smoothed around to my front and teased the band of my panties.

"Because kissing you, touching you, and pretending was the hardest thing I've ever acted."

"So, Dick, how about you take me back to your place?" I moved my hand around to his front and cupped his hard cock. "And we can put this dick to good use?"

"I love the way you think."

"And I love the way you make me feel." I caressed him through his pants as his fingers dipped inside my panties and found my slick, hard nub. "Oh, Valentine."

"Best Valentine's Day ever finding you," he said, stroking my damp flesh with a firm caress.

"Mine too," I gasped as he removed his fingers.

"Get dressed, then we can get out of here."

I stepped away from him and shimmied into my jeans and shirt.

He gathered my hand in his and asked, "Can I call you my girlfriend?"

I swooned a little harder than ever before, my knees wobbled, and my vision wavered. Valentine D. Ross asked if he could call me his girlfriend? Somebody pinch me. No, scratch that. If this was a dream, then I didn't want to wake up.

"Yes," I screeched.

He grimaced, but laughed.

"Can I call you my boyfriend?"

"Olive was right. You are loco."

"Hey." I pouted.

He dipped his head and kissed my pout away.

"If you're my girlfriend, then I'm your boyfriend."

"Perfect," I sighed.

And it was. He was. Everything about Valentine, Valentine's Day, and moving back to America was perfect. For the next eight weeks, I'd pretend to act in sex scenes with my boyfriend, who was the sexiest man alive. It didn't get more perfect. After the eight weeks were up, well, we'd figure that out then. For now, I'd enjoy life and everything in it.

I'd enjoy Valentine the most.
For the man was dream-worthy.
And this woman was living the dream.

Read Candy and Devin's story in How the
Grinch Lusted After Santa the first book in
the Hollywood Hearts series.

Read Olive and Tate's story in The
Lustful Leprechaun the third book in the
Hollywood Hearts series.

Afterword

Thank you so much for reading Lusting after Valentine. I hope you enjoyed this steamy Valentine's Day short story.

Did you love my story?
Review it!

A reader who writes a review for a book is a tremendous gift to the author. It lets me know that someone read my book and enjoyed the story enough to tell me. If you enjoyed this book, please leave a review on Amazon or GoodReads. I'd be forever grateful.

Acknowledgments

First, thank you to my family for putting up with me disappearing into the world of books. To Belinda, thank you for encouraging me to write again after I lost everything in a computer crash. Remember to back up! A lot of work goes into creating a story, and I'm always thankful for the support of my online writing buddies, beta readers, and fellow authors, Immy for always making me smile, Tammy for believing in me from the start, Karen for being willing to read any level of heat I write. Cassie for her hand holding. Lana for her invaluable knowledge. Also, my fabulous beta reader Erica and her help with US English. The biggest thank you goes to my 'twin' Dannielle, who is the best critique partner, cheerleader, and sounding board ever, and is forever fixing my comma errors, sorry Dannielle I'm afraid you're stuck with them and me. Finally thank you to all you romance readers. You are my tribe.

Also By

FANTASY AND PARANORMAL ROMANCE
Summer Court

Fae's Song

Fae's Wolf

Fae's Alpha

Fae's Heart

CONTEMPORARY ROMANCE
Billionaires' Reluctant Brides

Their Love Deal

His Pleasure Contract

Love Negotiations

Her Love Submission

Hollywood Hearts Short Stories

How The Grinch Lusted After Santa

Lusting After Valentine

The Lustful Leprechaun

The Lust Bunny

Anthologies

Reluctant Bride

Alpha Male

About Author

Helen Walton is a tea drinking, chocoholic, romance writer. Stories are her obsession. She adores creating sensual romances containing a sprinkling of humor and the all-important happy ending. She lives in South Australia with her family, and menagerie of quirky animals where they all take her away from her book world and demand to be fed. Lucky for them, she enjoys cooking but prefers baking.

Sign up for my newsletter for exclusive content.

https://www.helenwaltonauthor.com/newsletter
Visit my website

https://www.helenwaltonauthor.com/

Follow me

a amazon.com/author/helenwalton

BB bookbub.com/profile/helen-walton

f facebook.com/Helen-Walton-Author-103496667706602/

g goodreads.com/author/show/20249188.Helen_Walton

instagram.com/helen.walton.author

pinterest.com.au/HelenWaltonAuthor/boards/

tiktok.com/ZSJgrfgrC/

LUSTING AFTER VALENTINE